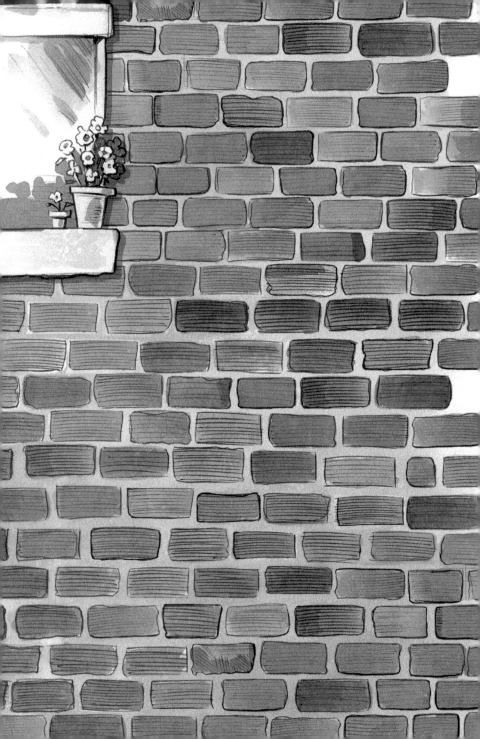

THE INFAMOUS RATSOS

Kara LaReau

illustrated by Matt Myers

CANDLEWICK PRESS

Text copyright © 2016 by Kara LaReau
Illustrations copyright © 2016 by Matt Myers

First edition 2016

Library of Congress Catalog Card Number pending
ISBN 978-0-7636-7636-0

16 17 18 19 20 21 BVG 10 9 8 7 6 5 4 3 2 1

Printed in Berryville, VA, U.S.A.

This book was typeset in Scala.
The illustrations were done in ink and watercolor.

Candlewick Press
99 Dover Street
Somerville, Massachusetts 02144

visit us at www.candlewick.com

For my grandfather,
the original Ralphie xo
K. L.

For Bruce,
my childhood coconspirator
in nefarious deeds
M. M.

HANG TOUGH

This is Louie Ratso. This is Ralphie Ratso.

The Ratso brothers live in the Big City. They live in this apartment with their father, Big Lou.

"There are two kinds of people in this world," Big Lou likes to say. "Those who are tough, and those who are soft."

Big Lou is tough, tough, tough. He drives a truck and a forklift and sometimes a snowplow. He hardly ever smiles.

As for the Ratso brothers' mother, she's been gone for a little while now, which is very sad. The Ratso brothers don't like to think about Mama Ratso. Big Lou doesn't like to think about Mama Ratso either.

"Hang tough," he grumbles each morning as he leaves for work, slamming the door behind him.

HATS OFF

After **Big Lou** leaves for work each morning, the Ratso brothers go to school. Louie is in the fifth grade and Ralphie is in third. They walk to school, because walking is tough. Taking the bus is for softies.

The Ratso brothers don't talk very much on their way to school. Talking a lot is also for softies. Their father hardly ever talks at all. Big Lou is a man of action, not words.

"Let's do something," Louie says to Ralphie. "Something to make us *look* tough."

"Like what?" Ralphie asks.

"Leave the thinking to me," says Louie. He considers himself the smart one.

At recess, Louie and Ralphie meet on the playground. They lean against the wall and glare at everyone and take turns spitting on the blacktop. Leaning and glaring and spitting are tough. Running and playing are for softies.

Chad Badgerton is wearing a new hat today. It is red, and it is too small for his head.

Louie has an idea.

"We'd look tough if we took Chad's hat," he suggests.

"Chad is bigger than we are," Ralphie reminds him. "A *lot* bigger."

"Well, there are two of us, and only one of him," Louie says.

"Righto," Ralphie says. He gives his brother a nod.

Ralphie distracts Chad while Louie jumps up and swipes the hat from his head.

"Hey!" cries Chad. "You can't do that!"

"We just did," shout the Ratso brothers. "Nyah-nyah!"

"I think I feel tougher," says Ralphie.

"My head is about to feel warmer, that's for sure," says Louie. But before he can put on the hat, Tiny Crawley comes running over, along with Miss Beavers, the third-grade teacher.

"You rescued my hat!" Tiny exclaims. He takes it from Louie.

"*Your* hat?" say the Ratso brothers.

"Chad took it from me on the bus," Tiny says. "He's a big bully."

"That was nice of you boys, sticking up for Tiny," says Miss Beavers.

"We're not nice, we're TOUGH," Louie tries to explain.

"Nyah-nyah!" Ralphie repeats.

But no one is listening. Instead, everyone on the playground is looking at the Ratso brothers like they're heroes. Everyone except for Chad Badgerton, who is on his way to the principal's office.

"I wish *we* were going to the principal's office," Ralphie says.

"We need to step up our game," decides Louie.

3

THE SNOW JOB

When the Ratso brothers wake up, it's snowing. Everything in the Big City looks like it's draped in white sheets.

"No school today, boys," says Big Lou. "The buses can't get down the roads."

"Buses are for softies," says Louie.

"I'm off to do some snowplowing," grumbles Big Lou. "Hang tough. And try not to get into too much trouble while I'm gone." He slams the door behind him.

"I have an idea," says Louie.

"How much trouble will it get us into?" asks Ralphie.

"Plenty," says Louie. "Let's go."

The Ratso brothers put on their snow pants and coats and gloves and boots and scarves and hats. They grab their shovels and go outside. It is still snowing.

"I can't see," says Ralphie. "What's the plan?"

"The plan is that we shovel all the snow from the sidewalk and pile it all up in front of Mr. O'Hare's store. When he comes down for work this morning, he won't be able to open the door!"

"That's mean," says Ralphie.

"That's *tough*," says Louie.

"Righto," Ralphie says, cracking his knuckles. "Let's make some trouble."

The Ratso brothers go out to the sidewalk and begin shoveling. They shovel and shovel and shovel, even when the snow starts falling so heavily they can't see a thing.

"This is hard work," says Ralphie.

"It will make us tougher," says Louie. "Keep shoveling."

"This way," says Ralphie.

"No, this way," says Louie.

"I'm pretty sure it's this way," says Ralphie.

"I'm pretty sure I'm the big brother," says Louie. "*This* way."

The brothers shovel and shovel until they can't shovel anymore. They fall back onto a snowdrift.

"I'm tired," Ralphie says with a yawn.

"Me, too," admits Louie. Soon the Ratso brothers are asleep.

"Why, you boys are as good as gold!" a voice exclaims.

"What?" says Louie. He nudges Ralphie awake.

Mr. O'Hare is in the doorway of his store, tears forming in his eyes. "It would have taken me all day to shovel that. I'm going to tell every one of my customers how thoughtful you are!"

"We're not thoughtful, we're TOUGH!" insists Louie. But Mr. O'Hare isn't listening; he's already open for business, with a little extra spring in his step.

"How did he get out?" asks Ralphie.

"We ended up shoveling all the snow away from Mr. O'Hare's door instead of *toward* it," Louie explains. "Somehow, we got turned around."

"Somehow?" says Ralphie.

"Don't worry," says Louie. "I'm sure another idea will come to me."

"Sure, *big brother,*" says Ralphie.

The Ratso brothers trudge home.

They spend the day shivering in front of the heater in their long johns, drinking hot chocolate.

4

THE
FLUFFY
SPECIAL

This is Florinda Rabbitski. She's just moved to the Big City," Mr. Ferretti announces to his students, including Louie.

"I like being called Fluffy," Florinda says meekly, looking at the floor.

"Her name sounds funny. And she looks weird," says Chad Badgerton.

At lunch, no one sits with Fluffy Rabbitski. She picks at her lunch of lettuce and raw vegetables and carrot juice. She seems sad, and lonely.

As always, the Ratso brothers sit together and eat their cheddar cheese sandwiches.

"Check out the new girl," says Louie.

"She smells like carrots," says Ralphie.

"Her name is Fluffy Rabbitski. She seems like a softie," says Louie. "Even her name sounds soft." He wrinkles his nose. And then he reaches into his brain and picks out another tough idea.

That night, before they go to bed, the Ratso brothers make their cheddar cheese sandwiches for the next day.

They also make a very special sandwich, piled high with the worst foods they can find in the refrigerator.

"Fluffy Rabbitski is in for a big, stinky surprise," Louie says.

At lunch the next day, Fluffy Rabbitski is about to sit by herself again when Ralphie gives her a whistle. Louie pats the seat next to him.

"Why don't you eat with us?" he suggests.

"Thank you," says Fluffy. She sits down and quietly takes out her sad little lunch of lettuce and raw vegetables and carrot juice.

"We thought you might like a real Big City treat," Louie says, pushing the sandwich in front of her. "We call it the Fluffy Special. We made it just for you."

Fluffy unwraps the sandwich and takes a sniff. Her eyes grow wide. Ralphie doesn't know whether to laugh or pinch his nose. The sandwich smells beyond awful.

But then Fluffy Rabbitski grabs the sandwich with both paws and takes a huge bite.

"Mmmmm," she says, swallowing. "Pickled mushrooms and beets and eggplant, just like my nana used to make! How did you know?"

"We didn't," Louie says. But Fluffy is too busy enjoying her sandwich to care. When she finishes, she pats her belly and looks at the Ratso brothers with shining eyes.

"I've been missing my old house and my nana since we moved here," she explains. "You two are the first to make me feel at home. I can't wait to tell everyone how generous you've been to me."

"We're not generous. We're TOUGH!" Louie insists. But Fluffy Rabbitski is not listening. She's licking her lips, still tasting that sandwich.

"Is this seat taken?" asks Tiny Crawley, sliding in next to Fluffy.

Louie throws up his hands.

"Maybe *I* should come up with the next idea," suggests Ralphie.

5

THE PORCUPINI WINDOW

On the way home from school on Friday, the Ratso brothers pass by Mrs. Porcupini's house. Mrs. Porcupini spends her days leaning against her cane and staring out her window with a sour expression on her face,

like she's just sucked on a pickle. She

seems to reserve her sourest looks for

the Ratso brothers.

Ralphie Ratso's brain is not quite as big as his brother's, but it is filled to the brim with ideas. He reaches in and pulls out a nasty one.

After Big Lou gets home and the Ratso brothers eat their dinner and wash the dishes and put them away and get into bed and turn out the light, Ralphie whispers his plan to his brother.

Then he says, "After tonight, everyone in the neighborhood will know how tough the Ratso brothers are."

They wait until they hear Big Lou's snoring, and then they sneak out of the apartment and down the stairs and outside. They creep over to Mrs. Porcupini's house. Ralphie reaches into his pockets and pulls out two big bars of soap.

"Let's teach that prickly pickle not to give us sour looks," he whispers. "When she looks out her window tomorrow morning, she won't be able to see a thing!"

"Pretty clever," says Louie. Though he still considers himself the smart one.

The brothers begin rubbing soap all
over Mrs. Porcupini's window. When
they're done, they have plenty of soap
left over.

"Let's keep going," says Ralphie.

The Ratso brothers soap each and every one of Mrs. Porcupini's windows. By the time they're done, the sun is coming up. Louie lets out a big, long yawn.

"Shhh!" says Ralphie.

But the sound has already woken up Mrs. Porcupini. She goes to the picture window and lets out a little yelp of surprise.

The Ratso brothers start running. But they've been awake all night soaping windows, so they're too tired to run very fast. And Mrs. Porcupini is already calling for them from her front porch, so they don't get very far.

"Louie and Ralphie Ratso!" she shouts. "Come here this *instant*!"

"We're really in trouble now," Ralphie says.

"Finally," says Louie.

When they climb the steps of the front porch, the Ratso brothers can

see that Mrs. Porcupini's sour-pickle expression is gone. In its place is an expression that looks very much like delight.

"I haven't been able to wash my own windows since I hurt my knee," Mrs. Porcupini explains. "It pains me to look out a dirty window. You boys saw someone in need and did something about it. I can't wait to tell everyone in the neighborhood how helpful you two are!"

"We're not helpful, we're TOUGH!" Ralphie insists.

But Mrs. Porcupini isn't listening; she is too busy showing them where the garden hose is and how to hook it up. The Ratso brothers spend the rest of the morning rinsing off all the soap until Mrs. Porcupini's windows sparkle in the sun.

- 6 -

"HE DID IT"

When they get home, the Ratso brothers want nothing more than to climb into bed and sleep all day. But that isn't going to happen. Because waiting for them in the kitchen is their father. In his hand is an open letter, printed on crisp white paper.

"This just came from the school," Big Lou says. "Do you boys have something you'd like to tell me?"

"He did it," the Ratso brothers say at the same time, each pointing at the other.

"You've both been busy. According to Mr. Ferretti, you welcomed a new student to the school and made her lunch. And according to Miss Beavers, you stopped a bully from terrorizing another student," Big Lou says, rereading the letter. "And then, this morning, when I went out to get the mail, Mr. O'Hare told me you two shoveled his sidewalk during the snowstorm."

"It was an accident," Ralphie tries to explain.

"Which part?" asks Big Lou.

"All of it," says Louie.

"So you're not really nice, or kind, or thoughtful, like everyone's saying?" Big Lou asks.

"No, and we're not helpful either, so don't listen to whatever Mrs. Porcupini tells you," Ralphie says. "We're TOUGH!"

"We just want to be like you," admits Louie.

"Like me?" says Big Lou.

"Yeah, you're tough. Being nice and helpful is for softies," says Ralphie.

Big Lou looks at the photo of Mama Ratso on the wall. He hangs his head.

"The last thing you want is to be like me," he says. "It's been hard on all of us since your mother's been gone. But you two have found a way to take care of yourselves and be good to others. *I* should be trying to be more like *you*."

Louie and Ralphie blink.

They look at the photo of Mama, too. They think about how soft and warm she was. And how good she was to them.

"Being tough all the time is so . . . so . . . *tough*," says their father. He puts his arms around the Ratso brothers and pulls them close.

"I think I have something in my eye," says Louie.

"Me, too," says Ralphie.

Before long, they are crying, Big Lou loudest of all.

TOUGH ENOUGH

This is Louie Ratso. This is Ralphie Ratso. This is Big Lou Ratso.

Everyone in the Big City knows the Ratsos. And everyone stays out of their way. Because who knows what they might be up to next?

They might just rake and bag your leaves for you on a windy day.

You might wake up one morning to see they've fixed your broken fence.

They might even push you on the playground swing.

"Life is tough enough," says Big Lou. "We might as well try to make it easier for one another, whenever we can."

"No worries. I've got big plans for us," says Louie. He still considers himself the smart one. So does Fluffy Rabbitski.

"Whatever your plans are, count me in!" says Fluffy.

"Whee!" says Tiny Crawley. "This is fun!"

"Righto!" says Ralphie.